About the Author

Barbara was born in Stow-on-the-Wold, Gloucestershire, and she lived all of her younger life in Cardiff. At the age of 22 she met her future husband, David, from Nottingham.
After moving to Nottingham, Barbara became involved in his underwear manufacturing and retail outlet business and gave birth to two children.
The couple moved back to Cardiff when they retired, which is where Barbara wrote her first story for children, entitled *The Snowman*.

Dedication

To Mrs Lynne Wilcox, my computer tutor, for her patience and encouragement.

Barbara Etherington Dilks

# THE SNOWMAN

A CIP catalogue record for this title is available from the British Library.


ISBN 9781786120502 (Paperback)
ISBN 9781786120519 (Hardback)


www.austinmacauley.com

First Published (2015)
Austin Macauley Publishers Ltd.
25 Canada Square
Canary Wharf
London
E14 5LQ




Printed and bound in Great Britain

# Chapter 1

In the county of Glamorganshire, South Wales, was the village of Marshfield, near Cardiff, not far away from the beautiful Wye Valley of Monmouthshire. Marshfield village had its own church, village hall, community centre, playing areas, lots of country walks with plenty of fishing ponds for children, and a good school. Although Marshfield had been expanding very quickly, it still held its peacefulness.

Stony Cottage was built deep in the countryside of Marshfield. It was an old, pretty, detached cottage made of stone. Over the years it had been extended and now had four bedrooms, a big lounge, a study, and a large kitchen-diner. In the back garden stood a large orchard, water fountain which lit up at night, a goldfish pond, plenty of hedges, flower beds and a couple of old barns. There were plenty of rare birds and squirrels that came to visit.

In the front garden were two very large lawns with lots of trees, all finished off with a narrow brick wall that went all the way around the property to the main wooden gate. At the end of the back garden you could see large woodland which gave Stony Cottage an air of mystery about it.

Holly, who lived in Stony Cottage with Mum and Dad, was six years old. She had deep set blue eyes, light brown curly hair and was a daddy's girl, a bit of a dreamer, good at art, and already in the school choir. Her younger brother, Zak, had darker brown hair with blue eyes like his sister. He liked dressing up as Batman, Spiderman and Robin Hood, and spent a lot of time playing football. After being in school for a few months he had settled in very well.

# Chapter 2

Zak loved the fish pond in the garden, which was full of goldfish. He would feed them every day with his dad before going to school.

Outside the cottage was a local bus stop, which took him and his sister to school, and also into Cardiff city centre. There were plenty of neighbours who would use the bus and could see into their front garden.

Zak always went fishing with his dad. They would go for long country walks and catch all sorts of creatures from the dykes. The dykes were there to stop the rain water from flooding the fields. There were plenty of horses and one or two would look out for them. There was always an apple, or carrot from Dad, and Zak would carry the bread to feed the ducks or the swans that were in the dykes.

Dad, who was called Robert, had his own garage business near Marshfield repairing cars, whilst Mum, Elaine, ran her own jewellery stall on the markets around the areas of Cardiff.

# Chapter 3

They were both in their early thirties and they were all very happy living at Stony Cottage. Robert and Elaine bought Stony Cottage from Elaine's mum and dad who had now retired, and were living in a small bungalow just around the corner not too far away.

Holly and Zak were looking forward to breaking up for their Christmas holidays. The last few months had turned very cold, winter had arrived and the snow had been falling for a few days.

Christmas was still a month away. Although the snow was settling, it had now stopped falling.

"Oh it would be nice to have a white Christmas," said Holly as she stamped some snow off her boots on the indoor mat after coming home from the playing area.

"Yes," replied Mum. "We may be lucky. It will soon be time to start on the Christmas decorations."

The following week Holly opened her bedroom curtains, and was surprised to see the snow had fallen very heavily in the night. It all looked very white and pretty.

"Look Mum!" she cried as Mum opened the bedroom door, "snow everywhere! We won't be able to go to school today!"

"No," said Mum, "there's no traffic getting through, we're all going to have the next few days off. If it stops snowing tomorrow, why don't we all build a snowman?"

"Yes!" cried Zak, who had just arrived from his bedroom wearing his pyjamas and had heard everything Mum had said, "I would love to build a snowman. Will Dad help?"

"Of course he will," smiled Mum.

Holly was delighted; "What a good idea Mum, we will have great fun making him and he will be the best looking snowman in Marshfield."

"We will build the snowman in the front garden, all our neighbours and friends will see him there," remarked Mum. "Then we must all decorate the house ready for Christmas."

The children were getting very excited about Christmas and this would be their first snowman at Stony Cottage.

# Chapter 4

The next day it had stopped snowing and they all went into the garden to build the snowman. As soon as the children saw the snow they could not resist playing snowballs. They were all laughing and fooling around in the snow having great fun.

After a few hours Mum laughed, "We must build the snowman, time is going, the men will make the body part and the girls will make the head."

It took quite a while to get the snowman into a good shape. They all worked very hard and eventually he was ready to be finished off with a hat and scarf. Zak wanted to fetch some stones to put on the snowman's face.

"Let's have a hot drink first to warm us up," said Mum. "Zak, then you can find an old hat and scarf. Holly you can search my button box for his eyes, and four different coloured big buttons for his coat, and I will give you a carrot for his nose."

It took Holly quite a long time to find two buttons the same size for the snowman's eyes. After placing them on the snowman's face, she put the buttons down his coat, and he looked really smart. She then placed the carrot that Mum gave her on his nose.

Zak had great fun making a great big smile on the snowman's face with his finger. Dad had to lift him up to reach. The snowman was taller than Holly.

Holly went to find more stones to finish the snowman's mouth. As she was searching around the bushes she heard a kitten cry. She looked under the bush and to her amazement she saw a black kitten.

"Goodness me, what are you doing in our garden?" cried Holly. The kitten meowed. Holly picked it up and ran into the house to show Mum.

"Look Mum, what I've found in the garden! Can I keep it?" she asked.

Mum looked quite surprised, "A kitten!" she cried. "Where on earth did you find it?"

"Under a bush," said Holly, "in our garden, I'm going to call it Lucky, can I keep it?"

"Well, we can't leave it out in the cold so it can stay with us until I find its owner from around the neighbourhood," remarked Mum, "I'll look after the kitten although I've never seen one with blue eyes before. Holly, you go and finish the snowman."

# Chapter 5

Holly told Zak about the kitten that she had found. "It was small, blue black fur with big blue eyes, cute soft and cuddly I'm going to call it Lucky," she said.

"Lucky?" Zak declared, "it won't be lucky if it catches our goldfish."

Zak had found an old coloured beret and scarf and with the help of Dad put them on the snowman. Holly then put the stones on for his mouth.

"There, the snowman is all finished. I hope he will stay with us now after all our hard work," said Holly.

"Of course, the snowman will melt away when the weather gets warmer," laughed Zak as he threw a snowball at his sister.

The following week everything went back to normal, traffic was getting through Marshfield, and the children were back in school. The snow had stopped falling although it was still very cold.

Every night when Holly came home from school she would ask the snowman to stay, and not melt away, "You're the best looking snowman in Marshfield." Then she told the snowman she would paint a picture of him in school and hang it on her bedroom wall, then she would always remember him. "Please don't melt away before Christmas," she said.

All the neighbours were talking about the snowman as they were waiting for the bus, saying how good he looked, and all the children loved him. He was quite the talk of the neighbourhood.

# Chapter 6

Soon the children would be breaking up from school for their Christmas holiday. All the decorations had been put up ready for Christmas. Holly had hung her painting of the snowman that she had done at school on her bedroom wall.

Dad had brought home a real big Christmas tree from the local market and the children helped him to decorate it, which took them quite a long time. When they had finished, the fairy lights were all switched on.

"Oh," gasped Holly, "now it does look like Christmas, the tree looks lovely, thank you Dad!"

Zak then placed all the presents for friends and family under the tree.

Both Mum and Dad went to the nativity play at the school. Zak was a shepherd, and Holly was in the school choir singing Christmas carols. Mum said they were both very good, so they could invite their friends for tea as they had broken up for the school's Christmas holidays.

# Chapter 7

Holly's friend was called Jasmine, and Zak had a friend called Brandon, who was Jasmine's sister. They came from the same school and they lived near Zak and Holly's grandparents, who lived around the corner, not too far away from Stony Cottage.

"We must see the snowman!" said Brandon, so they all went into the garden to play snowballs, and they had lots of fun with the snowman.

"I think the snowman is lovely," Jasmine shouted.

"I wish we had him in our garden," Brandon agreed. Then Holly showed them the kitten she had found in the garden.

"Lucky is his name," smiled Holly. "No one has claimed him so it looks like I can keep him."

After tea they played for an hour and then Jasmine and Brandon went home. The next day Holly was so pleased that the snowman was still outside.

"It will be Christmas in a couple of days, I hope the snowman will stay with us," groaned Holly.

"Now the weather is getting warmer, he may melt away," remarked Mum, "and there is nothing we can do."

No cried Holly, "I want him to stay."

"Well he will always be with you," beamed Mum. "You have his painting on your bedroom wall."

"Yes," Holly replied, and she felt glad at that moment she had painted the snowman's picture.

Christmas Eve had arrived. Lucky the kitten was playing with a trimming, Mum and Dad were both busy in the kitchen.

After playing most of the day with Zak, Holly put on her scarf and coat and went out to see the snowman.

"I've come to say goodbye," she said in a very sad tone, "it's Christmas Day tomorrow, you may melt away tonight."

So she promised the snowman that she would rebuild him when the snow came back and she would never forget him.

Zak could not get into bed quickly enough because it was Christmas Eve, and he was so excited about all his new toys. He had left a long list of presents he required from Father Christmas, and Holly had done the same, so between them they left a glass of milk and three biscuits for Santa.

As Holly jumped into bed she was feeling excited but very tired, it had been a busy day and her thoughts went to Lucky the kitten. Nobody had claimed him, so Mum said he could stay.

"What a wonderful Christmas present," she thought, and then fell asleep.

# Chapter 8

Now during the night a very strange thing happened. Holly was woken up by a bright blue light shining all over her bedroom.

"Why…" she wondered, "is my bedroom covered in blue light?"

She got up and moved quickly to the window. She could hear a noise coming from the front garden and she realised this was where the blue light was coming from. Opening the window, she could hear Zak's voice.

"Zak," she called out, "I'm coming down."

Dressing quickly she ran downstairs, then put on her boots, hat, scarf and coat and left the front door open rushing out into the front garden.

"What is going on Zak? Where is this blue light coming from?" and at that moment she looked for the snowman. "Where is the snowman?"

"Over there," shouted Zak pointing to the edge of the garden, "he's rolling around, the snowman has come alive and is rolling around the garden!"

"He can't be, he can't be!" protested Holly.

"Yes," repeated Zak, "he's over there."

At that moment the snowman had heard Holly's voice. He rolled over to where she was standing, and then he popped his head up right next to her.

"I thought I heard your voice Holly, it is so good to meet you at last, I have enjoyed all your little chats to me."

# Chapter 9

Holly was taken aback as she gasped with amazement. She looked at the snowman - he looked so different! He had a small nose and just an opening for his mouth, but in spite of all this he was still her snowman.

Holly, who was still in shock, had trouble finding her voice.

"You're alive you're alive!" she blurted out, "how can you be alive?"

"Because I am not your snowman," came the snowman's reply. "Your snowman has melted away. I am still here thank goodness, as you can see, and my name is Snowball, I have come from the blue side of the rainbow, that is why we are covered in blue light."

"Let me explain," said Snowball, "you have noticed I have been rolling around your front garden, I can also bounce around just like a rubber ball, look!"

To their amazment the snowman showed them both how he could bounce.

"And there is something else I can do, lie flat on the ground just like I have melted, let me show you."

To their surprise he lay flat on the floor and slithered around, and then, he sprang up again.

"The trouble is, when I arrived I lay flat on your snow in the garden and fell asleep. Next thing I knew I was pushed into your snowman. It was a good place for me to hide so I stayed in there, but now he has melted away so here I am!"

Snowball took a deep breath, "Holly and Zak, what you must understand is this, I am not your snowman, your snowman has melted way. I'm very sorry to say this to you both, he's melted away and he will never come back."

Zak blurtered out, "Why are you in our garden? and why have you not melted away like our snowman and where has the rainbow come from?"

"Questions questions, yes yes," said Snowball. "You have a right to know, I've come from the other end of the rainbow, my name is Snowball. I have come from the land of Forever and Ever, and I live and work for Father Christmas, you know, Father Christmas, who will be delivering your toys and presents on Christmas day. I needed a holiday, a rest, but now, I have to go back to work to the land of Forever and Ever.

"You come from the other side of rainbow?" Holly muttered very slowly.

"Yes" relied Snowball, "surely you've seen a rainbow before."

"Well of course," said Holly, "many times, but I've never spoken to a live snowman before."

At that moment Zak shouted out, "The land of Forever and Ever, Father Christmas!"

"Yes, yes," cried out Snowball, "my good friend Mr Flex is picking me up any time now. He's coming through the rainbow in the rainbow space shuttle to take me home, that is why the rainbow is here, to take me home!"

Zak then repeated himself "Why have you not melted away like our snowman?"

# Chapter 10

"Well, I am a snowman but I'm made up of a different type of snow from the land of Forever and Ever, your snow down here is very soft and it melts away, our snow is more flexible like a fine rubber, that is why I can roll, bounce and lie flat on the ground, so you see I can't melt away." And then he paused, "Thank goodness, although, I'm still quite soft to the touch. I like the cold weather and the warm, so do you understand, I'm not your snowman?"

"Yes," said Holly, "we understand, you don't melt away."

"Good," replied Snowball.

Holly could see what happened and understood what Zak and dad must have done. Then Holly looked up at the colours of the rainbow, although she was standing in the blue part of the rainbow, she could see all the colours, which were a beautiful sight, spread high across the sky.

Just at that moment a small blue space shuttle arrived right in front of them. The roof slid back and out stepped Mr Flex.

"Hello," smiled Mr Flex, looking amused as he came out through the space shuttle door. "I've come to take Snowball."

# Chapter 11

"I've come to take Snowball home back to Father Christmas."

Holly thought what an odd looking person he was; as tall as her, very thin with thick hair that looked like straw standing straight on top of his head. He had a blue suit on, and long boots that curled up at the toes.

"No!" cried out Holly. "Please stay with us Snowball, we want you to stay."

Mr Flex looked at Holly and Zak with amazement and shouted out, "Of course Snowball can't stay, he works for Father Christmas and he needs him now, otherwise all the girls and boys will not get their toys."

Zak called out "Father Christmas! I've always wanted to meet Father Christmas, can we come with you?"

Holly was very surprised to hear Zak's outburst but she agreed, if they could both meet Father Christmas, that would be a good idea.

Mr. Flex had a word with Snowball and told him Father Christmas was coming back this way to deliver the toys so he could bring the children back. Snowball was losing his patience so he agreed.

They all got into the rainbow space shuttle after Holly had closed the front door of the house. Snowball bounced into the front seat next to Mr Flex, and the children went through the side door. There was just enough room to queeze into the two back seats.

"Are you both warm enough?" asked Mr Flex. "It is very cold in the land of Forever and Ever,"

"Yes thank you," they both replied, looking around the space shuttle. "We're all wrapped up and we've got our boots on."

"Good!" yelled Mr Flex as he took control and started the motor. Then he pressed the switch and a transparent roof slid over them "I'm sure you'll like to see more of the rainbow and the stars, it is a wonderful sight for you to see."

"Oh thank you Mr. Flex, what a good idea!" shouted Holly, and off they went, flying straight through the blue side of the rainbow.

# Chapter 12

"Look!" cried Zak. "I can see our school, and where I go fishing with Dad!"

It was all blue but they could see all around quite clearly. As they went higher and higher all the colours of the rainbow spread out in front of them. It was a beautiful sight.

Holly looked up, she could see the stars in the sky, and felt she could stretch her arm out and touch them, they looked like diamonds in the sky. Just as she was admiring it all, Snowball turned his head right round to face them both and then started to explain all about his life.

# Chapter 13

He lived on Christmas Mountain in the land of Forever and Ever, which was part of Lapland, working for Father Christmas. He was in charge of all the reindeers and their sleighs and he had to make sure that all the toys were ready for delivery for Father Christmas to take all over the world. It was a very important job.

"We understand," said Holly. "Do you know the reindeers' names?"

"Yes of course," replied Snowball.

"I look after Rudolph, Dasher, Dancer, Prancer, Comet and Cupid, I love them all," smiled Snowball, "and I know they have all missed me!"

"Zak and I would love to meet the reindeers and Father Christmas," said Holly.

"Of course, you will meet them, you will also meet Mr Beam, who can throw out all different colour beams of light from the palms of his hands and from the top of his head, and you have met Mr Flex, who can stretch his arms and legs and his neck, and then there is Mr Flare, he is in charge of the hot air balloon which will fly us all up to Christmas Mountain."

Then Snowball took another deep breath. "We call them the Rainbow Clan, they're all involved working with the rainbow, the three of them wear blue suits to match the rainbow of course."

"Yes that's right!" said Mr Flex, moving his neck up and down, and he showed the children how he could stretch his arms out, saying, "I'm very flexible, what can you do Zak and Holly?"

# Chapter 14

Snowball butted in, "Zak can dress up in all different costumes, and play football. Holly has painted a picture of their snowman and it hangs on her bedroom wall, they're both very clever."

"When we land shortly in the land of Forever and Ever you will meet Mr Flare and Mr Beam, who will be surprised to see you. They will both take us up to Christmas Mountain to Father Christmas' Grotto in their hot air balloon," Snowball remarked.

"Oh I like the sound of that," burst out Zak, "we've never travelled in a hot air balloon before."

A few minutes later Mr Flex called out, "Hold on, we're coming in to land!"

Holly soon realised they had landed in a field of snow in the land of Forever and Ever. Zak was laughing at Snowball, who had bounced out of the space shuttle and was rolling around the field, "Come on Zak, race me across the field to the hot air balloon!" cried out Snowball.

Holly waited for Mr Flex to park the space shuttle in the shed. She could see it was a very large field.

"I'm glad I have my boots on," said Holly. The hot air balloon was in the distance, and as they walked over the field the blue light from the rainbow was fading and the night was getting darker as they walked further and further away from the rainbow.

Holly felt that the snow under her boots was very light. It was very easy to walk over and she seemed to be walking quite quickly so they soon caught up with Zak and Snowball.

# Chapter 15

Mr Beam and Mr Flare came to greet them. Holly noticed they all wore the same blue suits with the same turned up toes on their boots.

"Hello," said Mr Flare, "we were only expecting Snowball and Mr Flex. Who are you?"

Snowball then explained to Mr Flare and Mr Beam why the children were there and they both understood.

"What an adventure for you both, have you ever flown in a hot air balloon before," asked Mr Flare?

Holly looked at Mr Flare and noticed he was fatter than Mr Flex. He had no hair but there was something on the top of his head.

"No," replied Holly, "this is our first time," and she noticed the hot air balloon was blue in colour just like their suits, and it was very large.

"I'm sure you will be alright," smiled Mr Beam as they all stepped into the hot air balloon. "I shall light up the sky for you."

Then he showed them how good his lights were working. The lights were fixed on the palms of his hands and arms, and a great beam of light shone from the top of his head.

Zak thought it all looked rather good, then Mr Beam showed them all the different colours of lights he could produce, just like the rainbow. Zak whispered to Holly, "I think he's showing off."

Mr Flare went straight up into the entrance of the balloon, onto the platform and ignited the gas for the hot air balloon. Holly noticed he could spin his head right around just like Snowball, and he also carried a light on the top of his head.

"We're ready to go!" shouted Mr Flare. "All of you hold on!"

Off they went, flying through the air, travelling higher and higher, towards Christmas Mountain.

Mr Beam was flooding the sky with his lights, making it all look quite clear. They could see Christmas Mountain ahead and Snowball shouted out, "Father Christmas' Grotto is about half way up, look you can see some lights flashing from the grotto!"

Yes, Holly and Zak could just about see it, although they were still a long way away and as they came nearer and nearer to the mountain, *whoosh!* Something had hit the basket. But they all managed to hold on.

# Chapter 16

Mr Beam shone his lights the other side of the basket.

"What an earth was that?" shouted out Holly. "It looks like a witch flying on a broomstick with a cat on her back!"

"Oh don't worry," yelled out Mr Beam. "It's only Winnie the witch on her broomstick with her pet cat. The witches often fly around. They live halfway up Christmas Mountain. Unfortunately, Winnie lost one of her kittens a few weeks ago. She is very upset and angry. Witches' kittens are rare and very expensive and of course they have magical powers. That is why they sit on the broomsticks, I think she is going to the Caves of the Shadows perhaps to make a magic spell to find her kitten. The Caves of the Shadows are right up to the top and around the back of the mountain. She has a long way to go,"

"I think I might have found her kitten," remarked Holly. "When Snowball came down to our garden I came across a blue-black kitten under a bush with blue eyes which is very strange. Where I come from kittens' eyes are usually yellow. We have had this kitten a while, nobody has claimed it. I think it must belong to Winnie the witch, perhaps the kitten travelled down with Snowball when they came to visit Stony Cottage?"

"Well it sounds like the kitten that's missing, we will have to tell her the good news," smiled Mr Flex. Then he told. Mr Flare, "It would be a good idea to drop Snowball off first at the grotto, then we can travel to the back of the mountain and find the Caves of the Shadows."

"Oh yes!" cried out Zak. "Let's all go to the top of the mountain and see the witches make their magic spells."

Snowball was quite surprised. "Yes it was possible the kitten could have got into the space shuttle with me and Mr Flex. Don't worry, Mr Beam will sort it all out and I will see Father Christmas and explain the situation."

Holly felt glad that she had told them about the kitten but felt sad she would not see it again. They were now getting nearer and nearer to Christmas Mountain.

"We will be landing soon," shouted Mr Flare, "right outside Santa's Grotto." Holly could see, thanks to Mr Beam lighting the whole area. What a wonderful place it looked as they came nearer to the bright lights.

"It all looks magical," shouted Zak. "Look out! We're coming in to land!"

# Chapter 17

They all landed safely right by the entrance of Santa's Grotto with lights flashing, and fireworks zooming through the air into the sky.

"I must leave you now, this is where I work," explained Snowball. The children gave him a big hug and said goodbye.

As they were waving goodbye to Snowball he shouted out, "I will see you both when you leave for home with Father Christmas."

The hot air balloon suddenly rose up to go nearer the top of the mountain. They now needed to catch up to Winnie the witch and tell her the good news.

"She is heading for the Caves of the Shadows!" cried Mr Flex. "We will catch her there, she can fly very quickly on that broomstick of hers with the cat!"

Zak was getting excited. He loved the chase, and as Mr Beam shone his light to the top of the mountain Zak could see her.

"Look there she is!" shouted Zak, but alas, Winnie the witch was too quick and disappeared around to the back of the mountain.

"She's gone out of sight now!" said Zak.

"Never mind," smiled Mr Beam, who was enjoying showing off all his bright lights. "We're not travelling as fast so we can't catch up with her, we will have to find Winnie inside the Caves of the Shadows!"

As they were travelling Zak wanted to know all about the Caves of the Shadow, so he asked Mr Flex "Why was it called the Caves of the Shadows?"

"Well…" Replied Mr Flex, "all our shadows are in the cave. We don't have shadows in the land of Forever and Ever, they're all inside the Caves of the Shadows, and they are there to help make the rainbows, without them we would not have all the beautiful colours of the rainbow."

# Chapter 18

Holly was listening with great interest, "Is my shadow in the Cave of the Shadows and Zak's?" she asked.

"Yes," grinned Mr Flex, "but you will have them back when you get home. All the shadows of the world are in the Cave of the Shadows, it is their home.

"We have never heard of that before, it is all very interesting," replied Holly.

"There is a lot you don't know about the land of Forever and Ever, but I'm sure you will in time," remarked Mr Flex.

"The witches and their cats, why are they in the Caves of the Shadows?" asked Zak.

"The witches and their cats are always in the Cave of the Shadows, we need them and their magic spells to help the rainbows. Our rainbows are different, there are not the same rainbows like you have at home," Mr Flare butted in.

Now they were travelling nearer and nearer to the caves. "The trouble is," said Mr Flex, "without the rainbows we can't travel."

As the hot air balloon landed Holly realised how true that was, they needed the rainbows. They all got out of the hot air balloon and waited for Mr Beam to throw the lights over the Caves of the Shadows.

Holly could not believe how cold it was! Mr Flare stayed with the hot air balloon.

"Come on Holly and Zak, we'll soon find Winnie the witch," said Mr Flex. As Mr Beam shone his light over the cave, they could see a great big entrance; "This is where we have to go in," said Mr Beam as he shone the light through the hole that was the entrance to the Cave of the Shadows.

# Chapter 19

As they walked through the entrance they could see quite a lot of holes in the rocks with lots of big black ravens sitting on top. Holly felt it was a frightening place to be. Zak was too busy chasing very small lizards until Mr Flex caught him with his long arm and brought him back.

"Stay with us Zak, you must not take anything from the Caves of the Shadows," he remarked as they walked on.

Mr Beam shone the lights to the top of the cave. It was full of bats and cobwebs which were so long they nearly reached the floor.

As they got deeper and deeper into the cave Mr Beam switched off the lights. They could now see quite clearly all the shadows as they appeared to be moving around the cave.

The shadows were flying into the circle of shadows, which were lying deep into the floor of the cave and spinning very fast. Suddenly they could hear this deep loud voice coming through the Cave of the Shadows.

"Who are you? What do you want?"

This large white shadow appeared on the side of the cave and shook itself right in front of them, and then it spoke with flashes of rainbow coloured lights coming from it.

"I am the Dean of the Shadows who are you what do you want?"

"It's only us, Mr. Flex and Mr Beam from the Rainbow Clan, we've come to find Winnie the witch to tell her we have found her kitten, and I am with Zak and Holly who come from the other end of the rainbow, Stony Cottage, which is where the kitten is. Father Christmas will be bringing the kitten later tonight."

# Chapter 20

Holly and Zak stood very quiet. They were amazed at what they were seeing, they could not make out whether the white shadow was speaking. The Dean of the Shadow was very pleased with the news and thanked Holly and Zak for the kitten. The kitten was very important and was needed for all of its magic powers.

"I will send Winnie the witch to you."

Then all the shooting colours stopped flashing and the Dean of the Shadow disappeared.

Winnie the witch soon appeared with her daughter, La La, who was also a witch.

"Hello Mr Flex, this is good news, I am so pleased you found the kitten."

"Yes," replied Mr Flex, "thanks to Holly and Zak, who come from Stony Cottage the other end of the rainbow." Winnie asked Zak and Holly if they would like to look around the Caves of the Shadows on their broomsticks.

"Yes that would be great," replied Holly and Zak, so they jumped on the broomsticks and away they went, flying through the caves.

Holly went with La La and Zak with Winnie, what a wonderful ride.

All over the caves they saw the witches stirring their pots and heard all the magic spells, listen to them singing and dancing.

They saw all around the computer rooms and had a look at all the Christmas toys that were being made for the boys and girls for Christmas.

It was such a busy place with lots of dwarfs darting here there and everywhere. Flying on the way back they could see all the shadows spinning so fast inside a big deep hole on the floor of the cave, trying to make the rainbows.

"That was a lovely ride, thank you," they both said when they arrived back to Mr Flex.

Holly and Zak waved good bye to Winnie and La La.

Mr. Flex and Mr Beam were delighted that the children had been around the Caves of the Shadows, perhaps they would understand more about the land of Forever and Ever.

"We must go now," said Mr Flex, so they all went to find Mr Flare, who was waiting by the hot air balloon.

"We must get to Santa's Grotto!" cried out Mr Flare. Soon they were all flying through the air in the hot air balloon. Holly and Zak were so excited after going around the Caves of the Shadows on the witches' broomsticks that they told Mr Flare all about it.

Mr Flex explained to Holly that she would receive another kitten in exchange for Lucky, and it would be the same age and colour, in fact you would not believe they had been swapped.

As they landed outside Santa's Grotto, Holly was so pleased to have the kitten exchanged, and that Father Christmas would bring a new one to her.

# Chapter 21

Mr Flare and Mr Beam stayed with the hot air balloon. Holly and Zak thanked them and said good bye. Mr Flex took both the children to find Father Christmas.

As they walked through the entrance of the grotto they could see all the decorations.

Zak pointed to the reindeers, "Look there are all Santa's reindeers!"

# Chapter 22

"Yes," said Mr Flex, "this is where Snowball works."

"What does he do?" remarked Zak.

"His job is to keep and look after the reindeers and make sure all the toys are in the sleighs ready for delivery for Father Christmas to go all round the world! He can roll faster than you can run, and bounce, and not to forget, he can slide. The dwarfs do most of the work, but snowball has the voice, he can shout louder than anyone in the land of Forever and Ever to make sure the job is done!" said Mr Flex.

"I see," answered Zak.

"Come on," said Mr Flex. "We will go and find Father Christmas on the train through Santa's Grotto."

# Chapter 23

All the fireworks and bright lights were shining through the sky. There were hundreds of Christmas trees all sparkling in the night, and lots of toys glittering. It really was a wonderful sight

Holly was so pleased to see it all. "Oh! I wish it was Christmas all of the time!" she shouted out to Mr Flex.

"Wow!" cried Zak, "this is all magical."

The train pulled in to Santa's Grotto. "Now we must find Father Christmas!"

Mr Flex knocked the door and Holly was surprised to see two black shadow fairies. They were half her size in height and very thin. Their wings were very pretty, glittering with the colours of the rainbow when they caught the light.

The fairies told Mr Flex that Snowball had been in touch and explained everything. Father Christmas would take the children home with their toys.

Then the fairies introduced themselves to the children. "We know you're Holly and Zak, my name is Dot and this is Spot," they said.

"I think those names really suit you," said Holly.

Mr Flex butted in, "I must leave you now, I'm going to sort your kitten out Holly. I will see you later with Father Christmas, the fairies will look after you, good bye Holly and Zak."

"You must come from the Shadows of the Caves," said Holly.

"Yes," said Dot. "We help Father Christmas to deliver all the toys around the world. We can slide through anything, doors, windows, even cracks, and we're very good at carrying the toys."

Zak thought they were very clever. Dot and Spot soon found Father Christmas having a cup of tea and biscuits, dressed in his usual red and white suit.

"Hello Holly, Hello Zak, I don't get visitors very often. Come and have a cup of tea and then you can tell me about all the toys you want for Christmas."

He bent down and picked them both up and balanced the children, one on each knee.

"Snowball has told me all about you," smiled Father Christmas. They both whispered in Santa's ear and told him which toys they wanted.

"Ho ho ho," he laughed. "We'll have to wait and see. I will sort out your kitten Holly, thank goodness Winnie will have it back."

The children were having great fun with Father Christmas, but now it was time to leave.

"Are the fairies coming with us?" asked Zak

"Yes," replied Santa, "now you will be travelling home in the red side of the rainbow, it is not as cold as the blue side, the red side is my part of the rainbow and it takes me anywhere I want to go."

"Can we meet the reindeer?" asked Holly.

"Of course you can," said Santa.

Soon they were outside the Grotto, the reindeers were waiting patiently and they could see the sleighs were full of toys ready for delivery.

# Chapter 24

As they approached the reindeers, everything looked red due to the colour of the rainbow. Father Christmas introduced the children to the reindeers.

"This is Rudolph with the red nose, and here is Dasher, Prancer and Dancer, and then we have Comet and Cupid. These are the reindeers that will be travelling with us pulling all the toys," he said.

Holly and Zak made a fuss of all of the reindeers as they were really pleased to see them. Dot and Spot sat with the toys on the sleigh ready to help Father Christmas.

Snowball had come to say goodbye, as had the Rainbow Clan, Mr Beam, Mr Flare, and Mr Flex. The children were so pleased to see them all once again and after a big hug, thanked them for a wonderful time and said they would never forget them all. Soon they were sitting next to Father Christmas on his sleigh, waving goodbye. It was sad to leave but Holly felt she would see them all again.

"I hope we will see you again Snowball!" shouted out Holly.

"Of course you will!" yelled back Snowball. "And don't forget you have your snowman painting on your bedroom wall!"

Off they went, leaving the land of Forever and Ever behind. As they travelled through the rainbow at great speed, they could hear Snowball shouting out, "Goodbye Holly goodbye Zak!"

The reindeers looked as if they were running, yet they were flying higher and higher through the red side of the rainbow.

Then Father Christmas told them both how good the fairies were and how he could not manage without them.

"I think it all has been wonderful!" said a very tired Zak.

In no time at all the reindeers had landed outside their home. They gave Santa a hug and said goodbye to him and the fairies.

# Chapter 25

Holly opened the front door of the house and noticed the red glow of the rainbow all over the stairs, and she thought what a wonderful time they'd both had in the land of Forever and Ever. Now they were very tired and soon they were both tucked up in bed fast asleep.

The next morning was Christmas Day, Holly woke up, got dressed and she could see all her presents in her bedroom, but there were more important issues to sort out.

She ran down into the kitchen and there was the kitten, "Lucky! You're still here thank goodness!" she smiled.

Then she noticed the kitten eyes were not blue, but yellow. She went into the garden to see the snowman, but he had melted away. All that was left was a hat, scarf, buttons and a few stones. Then she heard Mum's voice.

"Are you alright Holly? You have over slept. Why are you not opening your presents? I'm afraid the snowman has melted away. Never mind, we can build him again next year."

"Yes Mum, but you don't understand, we had another snowman called Snowball who was here last night from the land of Forever and Ever."

And then she told her mum all that happened in the night.

Holly picked up snowman hat, scarf, button and all the stones. Her mum looked quite shocked.

"Holly!" she said, "you have been dreaming. No wonder you have over slept."

"No, no," cried Holly. "Zak was with me, he will tell you all about it!"

She rushed upstairs with all the snowman's belongings and found Zak playing with his new toys.

"Zak! Zak! Tell Mum." Mum was right behind her.

Zak looked puzzled. "I don't know what you mean."

"Tell Mum all about the rainbow and Snowball and Mr Flex. We both went in the space shuttle up the rainbow to the land of Forever and Ever to meet Father Christmas."

"No, No, I don't understand, what are you talking about? I have not been to see Father Christmas. I want to play with my toys!"

"Holly, you have been dreaming," remarked Mum. "Come and open your presents."

Now Holly knew she had not dreamed this dream, everything was true. Why was Zak being so difficult, surely there was no harm in telling mum what happened?

Dad, who had been listening to all this, explained to Holly, "Dreams often seem so real that we all sometimes think they're true. I think you should go to your room and open your presents, after all Holly, it is Christmas Day."

Carrying the snowman's belongings, she went to her room and looked at the snowman painting on her bedroom wall. She told him she would build him again next year, and then she put all the snowman's things in a carrier bag and put them on the top of her wardrobe.

Why was Zak being like this? She could not believe he was doing this to her, he must remember. How could it all be a dream? It was all real and she knew she would see Snowball again.

Was it a dream? Holly's kitten had yellow eyes. Would she see Snowball and the rainbow again?

Hmm… That could be another story…